MY MOM
AND
OUR DAD

ROSE IMPEY & MAUREEN GALVANI

VIKING

VIKING

Published by the Penguin Group
27 Wrights Lane, London W8 5TZ, England
Viking Penguin, a division of Penguin Books USA Inc.
375 Hudson Street, New York, NY 10014, USA
Penguin Books Australia Ltd, Ringwood, Victoria, Australia
Penguin Books Canada Ltd, 2801 John Street, Markham, Ontario, Canada L3R 1B4
Penguin Books (NZ) Ltd, 182–190 Wairau Road, Auckland 10, New Zealand

Penguin Books Ltd, Registered Offices: Harmondsworth, Middlesex, England

First published 1990
10 9 8 7 6 5 4 3 2 1

Text copyright © Rose Impey, 1990
Illustrations copyright © Maureen Galvani, 1990

Filmset in Baskerville

Made and printed in Italy

ISBN-0-670-83663-X

The worst thing about my mom is...

She's always rushing,

calling,

shaking,

pulling,   pushing.

She drags me out of bed at eight. It's . . .

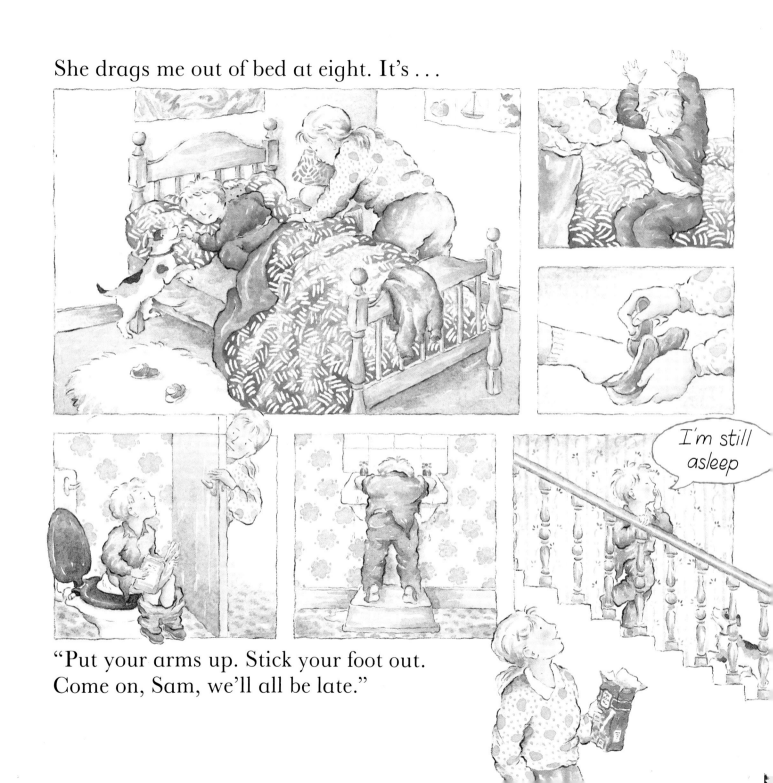

I'm still asleep

"Put your arms up. Stick your foot out.
Come on, Sam, we'll all be late."

At breakfast Mom says, "Don't be slow.

Sam, eat your toast. Sam, drink your milk.

Still eating

Sam, please be quick, it's time to go."

We race . . . . to get . . . .

She heaves . . . . and . . . . tugs . . . .

We're late . . . . The clock . . . .

to school . . . . on time. . . . .

. . . . . . I pant . . . . and . . . . puff.

. . . . begins . . . . to chime. . . . .

I hate it, shopping with my mom.

She zips in here, then zooms in there.
I drag behind and suck my thumb.

We're home at last, she still won't stop. It's ...

"Eat your beans up. Drink your juice, please. Sam, you haven't had a drop."

But at two o'clock the doorbell rings. It's Jane!

Mom . . .

can we paint?

Go swimming?

Will you push us on the swings?

I'm drinking my tea

Mommy – don't sit down just yet!

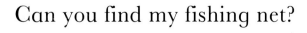

Where's my jacket?
Where's my bucket?

Sam, I'm tired

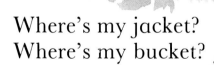

Can you find my fishing net?

Come on, Mom, we want a drink,
balloons and sweets, a party with treats...
Can we play boats in the sink?

The worst thing about that Sam is . . .

He's always rushing,

He never stops!

calling,   shaking,   pulling, pushing.

There's just one thing wrong with our dad . . .

He doesn't like teasing,

fighting   and fooling,

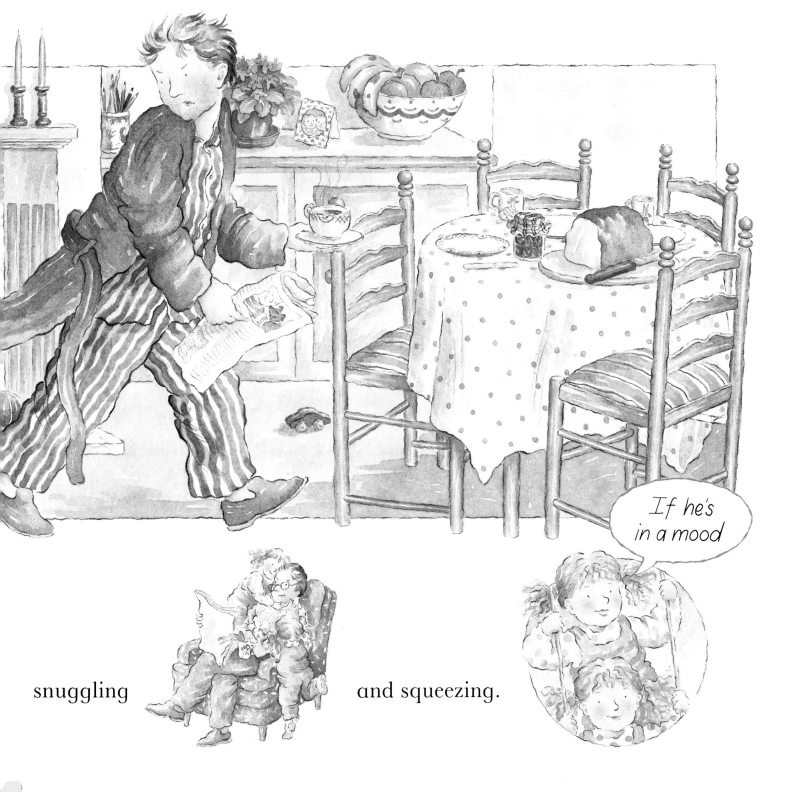

snuggling   and squeezing.

If he's in a mood

When he wakes up . . .

we climb in bed. "Don't jump," he moans. "Don't bounce," he groans.

"Will you two girls get off my head!"

It's like a circus

At breakfast time we mess about.
We stir, we swish, we flood the dish!
Our dad looks up. He starts to shout.

Dad works all day – it isn't fair.

We wave and call, we shout and bawl.

It's like a football match

He tells us off, "You rowdy pair."

We're dressing up; Dad's on the phone.
I start to wiggle and then we giggle.
"Clear off," he says. "Leave me alone."

It's like a pantomime

We're playing cars. Dad, come and see!

It's like a racetrack

We rrrev,   we hmmm,   we brum, brum, brrrmmm.

Dad nearly trips – he glares at me.

But later, when *he* wants to play
and we're twisting, twirling, wheeling, whirling . . .

You watch – he'll soon get carried away.

He picks us up and carries us off,
squawking and squealing up to the ceiling.
"3–2–1 . . . We have Blast Off!"

Then he tucks us in.
"That's one. That's two."

He crawls, he creeps, he taps, he peeps.

He tiptoes in and goes "Whoooooooo!"

There's just one thing wrong with those girls . . .

They don't like teasing,

When they
in a moo

fighting and fooling, snuggling and squeezing.